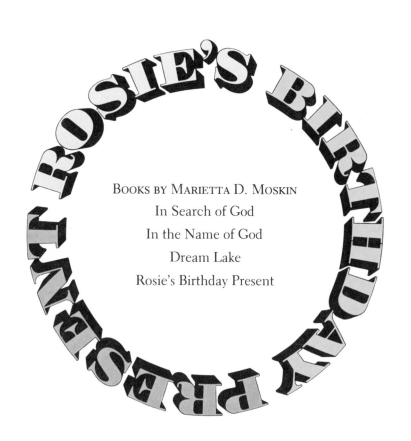

Books by Marietta D. Moskin

In Search of God

In the Name of God

Dream Lake

Rosie's Birthday Present

ROSIE'S BIRTHDAY PRESENT

by Marietta D. Moskin

pictures by David S. Rose

ATHENEUM   1981   NEW YORK

LIBRARY OF CONGRESS CATALOGING IN PUBLICATION DATA

Moskin, Marietta D.
Rosie's birthday present.

SUMMARY: Rosie trades many things until she finally
gets the right gift for her mother's birthday.
[1. Gifts—Fiction.   2. Birthdays—Fiction]
I. Rose, David S.   II. Title.
PZ7.M849Ro   [E]   81–2220
ISBN 0–689–30854–X   AACR2

Published simultaneously in Canada by
McClelland & Stewart, Ltd.
Printed in the United States of America
by The Connecticut Printers, Hartford, Connecticut.
Bound by A. Horowitz & Son/Bookbinders, Fairfield, New Jersey.
First Edition

IT WAS JUNE 7TH. Mamma's birthday.

Maria reminded Rosie in the morning.

"Don't forget. We'll have a party tonight when Mamma comes home from work," she said.

"But I have nothing to give Mamma," Rosie said.

Maria picked up her school books. "Don't worry," she said. "Mamma won't expect a present from you. Just give her an extra big hug."

Rosie didn't think a hug was enough of a birthday present. Everyone else in the family had prepared a surprise for Mamma. Carlos, who worked as a delivery boy after school, had saved his money and bought Mamma a silk scarf. Maria had spent hours embroidering Mamma's initials on two pretty handkerchiefs. Even seven-year-old Manuel had made a birthday card crayoned with hearts and flowers, and he had copied a poem for Mamma inside.

Rosie was not quite five. She had no money, and she couldn't sew or write. She didn't even draw very well. Besides, Manuel wouldn't ever lend her his school crayons.

It wasn't fair!

Tonight, when the others brought Mamma their gifts, Rosie would have to come with empty hands.

5

All day Rosie worried about Mamma's birthday. She worried while she ate her breakfast. She worried while she got dressed. She still worried about it when she went down the hall to stay with Mrs. Lopez, who looked after Rosie while Mamma was at work.

Rosie tried to talk about it with Mrs. Lopez. But Mrs. Lopez didn't have any ideas either. She was busy with her housework. Sometimes she played games with Rosie or she'd take her along to the stores. But today Mrs. Lopez was sewing new curtains for her kitchen. She had no time to listen to Rosie's problems.

"It's nice outside," she said after lunch. "Go and play in front of the house. Just stay where I can watch you from the window."

Rosie went down the four flights of stairs and sat on the steps in front of the house. Maybe when Maria came home from school, she'd help Rosie find a present. It was always such a long wait until school was over. Rosie sighed and settled down on the top of the steps. She hoped that her sister would hurry home from school today.

Suddenly something bright and shiny caught her eye. It was right below her at the bottom of the steps. A small, round, gleaming thing that caught the sunlight and bounced it back. Among the bits of broken glass and scraps of paper heaped around the crumbling steps, it shone like a piece of gold.

Rosie darted down the steps and reached for the shiny treasure. It was a button—a round gold button with raised designs carved around the edge. It was the prettiest button Rosie had ever seen.

Rosie held the button in the palm of her hand. What would she do with it? Then she smiled. Of course! She'd give it to Mamma. It would make a beautiful birthday gift. Rosie would polish it until it sparkled even more. Then Mamma could sew it on her good navy dress that had only a simple cloth button at the neck. How nice Mamma would look with that gold button to brighten her dress!

Rosie was still admiring her treasure when she felt someone poking her shoulder. She looked up to find her friend Mr. Muldoon smiling down at her. Mr. Muldoon was the mailman on the block. He often let Rosie make the rounds with him.

"Hey, what's the matter? Don't you have a smile for me today?" Mr. Muldoon asked. "I already did two houses all by myself. How about some company?"

"I'm sorry, Mr. Muldoon," Rosie said. "I have to go and polish my birthday gift for Mamma. Look, isn't it beautiful?"

"Say, where did you find that button?" Mr. Muldoon asked. "That must be the one I lost from my uniform. I noticed it only this morning."

He pointed to two little threads dangling from the top of his pocket flap. Sure enough, there were gold buttons just like Rosie's all over Mr. Muldoon's uniform. Small ones and big ones—all shiny, and all with exactly the same design.

Rosie felt her lip tremble. "But I need it for Mamma—for her birthday," she said.

Mr. Muldoon scratched his head under his cap. He was thinking hard.

"Now let's see," he said. "I need that button, Rosie. But perhaps we can find something else for your mother."

He searched through his pockets.

"Now here is something," he said. "What about this ballpoint pen?"

He pulled a long, thin, silvery pen from his inside pocket. He worked the button on it twice to show Rosie how the pen point would snap in and out. "Do you think your Mamma would like that, Rosie?" he asked.

Rosie thought the pen was beautiful. She turned it around and around in her hands.

"What does the writing on it say?" she asked.

"It says 'Compliments of Bill's Car Wash'," Mr. Muldoon said quickly. "Well, Rosie, is it a trade?"

"It's a trade," Rosie said. A pen was better than a button. She'd wrap it in tissue paper, and it would be a real gift for Mamma.

Holding the pen tightly, Rosie made the rounds with Mr. Muldoon to the end of the block.

"Goodbye, Rosie. Have a nice birthday party tonight," Mr. Muldoon said when they parted. Rosie headed back to her own house.

Halfway home she met another old friend. Policeman Sylvester was standing by a parked car at the curb. He was hurriedly searching through all his pockets.

"Did you lose something, Mr. Sylvester?" Rosie asked politely. She usually talked to Policeman Sylvester whenever he made a stop in her block.

"My pen gave out," Officer Sylvester grumbled. "Just when I wanted to write a ticket for that car parked right in front of a fire plug."

"You may use the pen I'm giving my Mamma for her birthday," Rosie offered.

Officer Sylvester quickly filled in the blank spaces on his ticket pad.

"That's a great pen," he said. "I wish it were mine. I sure could use it today."

He started to hand the pen back to Rosie. Then he paused.

"Say, do you suppose your Mamma might like a key chain with a flashlight instead of a pen?" he asked. He reached into his pocket and showed Rosie a small gold key ring with a narrow little penlight dangling from it on a gilded chain.

"It's quite new," Officer Sylvester said. "Someone gave it to me, but I'm still using my old one."

Rosie couldn't keep her eyes off the little chain.

"Do you really want to trade?" she asked. She was sure that Mamma would love to have that pretty key ring.

"Tell your Mamma happy birthday from me, too," Officer Sylvester said with a smile.

Rosie turned and almost bumped into a man who was standing at the curb, tinkering with something under the hood of a bright yellow taxi.

"Something's wrong," the cab driver muttered. "If I could only see what I'm doing in here. It's in such a dark spot."

Rosie peered curiously under the hood. "Want to use my flashlight?" she offered.

Without a word the driver reached for it and shone the light into a deep corner way in the back.

"There it is," he said. "There's the trouble. Just a loose wire, that's all."

He came out from under the hood and smiled at Rosie.

"Lucky thing you just came by with that handy flashlight. I sure could use a thing like that to keep my car keys on."

Once again Rosie explained about Mamma's birthday, and about all the trades she had made.

"I wish I had something to trade you for that flashlight." The cab driver sighed. He looked into his cab.

"Hey, wait!" he said. "I have just the thing for a birthday party. Some children left these in my cab yesterday afternoon."

He reached in and brought out a little shopping bag. Inside was a jumble of party favors: a red, white and blue paper hat with silver stars; a yellow and red blower; and a silver horn with red and blue ribbons.

Rosie tried out the blower. It uncurled into a long, thin, sausage shape and then snapped back with a satisfying plop. She tried it again.

Should she trade? It was a hard decision. Mamma already had a key chain. The party favors would turn dinner tonight into a real birthday party. Rosie could almost picture Mamma at the kitchen table, wearing the paper hat and blowing into the horn. Surely Mamma would prefer the party hat to the key chain. Rosie knew what she would pick if she had the choice.

"I'll trade," she said. She took the little paper bag and started skipping toward home.

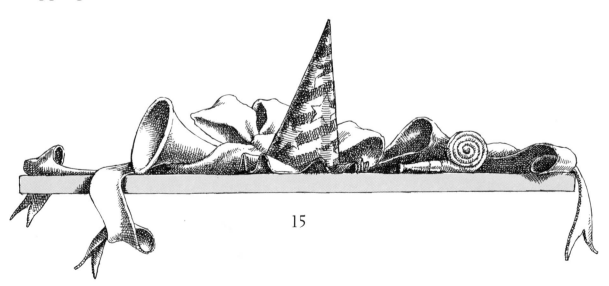

Just then she saw her old friend Joe, far down the block. Joe was the neighborhood Good Humor man. Rosie always stopped to chat with him.

Today Joe looked sad. "Hello, Rosie," he said sighing. "I sure have troubles today. The bell on my truck has a crack, and now I can't let the people know that I'm passing through. My voice isn't loud enough to get their attention."

"Maybe I can help you shout," Rosie said, "as soon as I take Mamma's birthday present upstairs." She showed Joe her collection of party favors. She tried the blower again. Then she blew into the horn. The sound that came out was loud. Very loud.

Above them, several windows opened.

"Hello, Good Humor man," a lady shouted from the third floor. "My boy is coming down with money for two chocolate crunch sticks. Make sure you give him some napkins, too."

"Two chocolate crunch sticks coming up," Joe called back with a smile.

"That sure is a loud horn," Joe said to Rosie. "It's almost as good as my bell. Look, business is picking up right away."

He looked into his truck.

"I wish I could keep that horn for today," he said. "But I have nothing to trade you for it except ice cream. Perhaps you'd like to celebrate your Mamma's birthday with an ice cream sandwich for everyone."

Rosie didn't know what to say. Ice cream sandwiches were a special treat. She could almost taste the sweet, cool chocolaty flavor on her tongue.

If she traded the horn, she'd still have the hat and the blower. And ice cream for dinner would be a real party surprise.

"I'll take the ice cream," she said quickly. "But I need one for Carlos, one for Maria, one for Manuel, one for Mamma and one for myself."

Joe put five ice cream sandwiches into an empty cardboard box.

"Have a nice party," he said. "And hurry home with that ice cream. It's pretty warm this afternoon."

He drove down the block, blowing his horn loudly.

Rosie turned toward home, holding the box carefully in both hands. But before she could go upstairs, there was something else she had to stop and see. The garbage truck had made its daily stop right in the middle of the block. Rosie just couldn't pass by without watching at least one load of garbage being chewed up by the huge crusher blades. She leaned against the fire hydrant and watched the garbage disappear into the insides of the great big truck.

The garbage men lifted up four more big garbage cans and emptied them into the hungry jaws of the machine.

Crunch, crunch, went the blades, and another load of garbage disappeared from sight.

Rosie loved to watch. She didn't want to leave until all the garbage cans were empty.

21

First Baptist Church
Child Care Center

Suddenly she felt something dripping down her left leg. Something cold. Something sticky.

"My ice cream!" Rosie cried. "It's melting. I'll have to get it to the icebox fast."

One of the garbage men laughed. "I'd say it's too late for that, young lady," he said. "Look, its running down the other side too. You'd better eat that ice cream now before you have nothing left but ice cream soup."

"But they're for Mamma's birthday dinner," Rosie whispered. She felt awful. How could she stand here and eat five ice cream sandwiches and then have nothing left for Mamma and Maria and the others.

"It was my special treat for Mamma's birthday," she explained to the garbage men. And then she told again about all of her trades.

"That's too bad," said the big man whom the others called Tom. "But I have an idea. Why don't we all have one of the ice creams now—it's so hot, I could use a cool snack. And then we'll find another present for your Mamma."

It seemed like the right thing to do. Rosie gave an ice cream sandwich to each of the men. She kept the fifth one for herself. It was pretty messy and gooey by now, but it tasted good anyway.

"Now for the gift," Tom said. "Look, I saved this for my wife, but you can have it for your mother. Imagine, someone threw this out!"

From behind the driver's seat he pulled out a small round mirror in a carved gold frame.

"The glass is cracked a bit." Tom showed Rosie. "But it still has lots of use in it."

"It's lovely." Rosie sighed. She could just see Mamma putting on her hat in front of this pretty mirror, hanging by the kitchen door. Mamma would surely be pleased with this special gift.

She waved goodbye to the garbage men and started up the steps of her house. Suddenly she heard someone yelling. Mrs. Dickey, the lady in the second-hand shop at the corner, was running down the street, waving her arms.

"Stop, stop!" she cried. "Someone help me stop that garbage truck. They took something by mistake."

"They just turned the corner," Rosie said helpfully. But Mrs. Dickey had stopped running. She was looking at the mirror Rosie held in her hands.

"Rosie, where did you find it?" Mrs. Dickey gasped. "My goodness, how lucky! You saved my little mirror. It didn't get crushed in the garbage truck."

Mrs. Dickey reached out and took the mirror from Rosie.

"But it's mine!" Rosie cried. "The garbage men traded me for it. Please don't take it away. I need it for my Mamma!"

And then Rosie couldn't help it. She started to cry. She had traded so many things that afternoon. Now it would all be for nothing. Mrs. Dickey would take her mirror back, and Rosie would come to dinner empty-handed after all.

Mrs. Dickey looked concerned. "Hey, don't cry, honey," she coaxed. "Tell me what this is all about."

Rosie told her. She started with the button and went on to tell about all the other trades. When Rosie had finished, Mrs. Dickey gave her a hug.

"Come to my store, Rosie," she said. "I can't let you have the mirror because it is quite valuable. I had put it on the floor to have it fixed, and the boy who works for me made a mistake and put it out with all the trash.

"But I'm sure I'll find something pretty in my shop for your Mamma."

27

It was dark in the little store, which was full of tables and chairs, vases and clocks, pictures and mirrors. Rosie looked around while Mrs. Dickey searched in a big drawer for something she could give to Rosie.

"Here it is," she said at last. "This is what I've been looking for."

She held out a small heart-shaped pin made of silver and set with a lot of tiny red stones.

"Do you like it?" Mrs. Dickey asked. Rosie could only nod yes. She was too excited to talk. She watched as Mrs. Dickey found a small blue box and lined it with soft yellow cotton wool. She nestled the pin in the bed of cotton and put more of the fleecy stuff on top. Then she wrapped the whole box in a small piece of bright red paper and tied it with a shiny piece of satin ribbon.

"I hope your Mamma will have a happy birthday," Mrs. Dickey said when Rosie left, her cheeks hot with excitement.

That evening, when Mamma came home from work, they all gathered around the kitchen table. One by one they gave Mamma their gifts. Mamma admired the red silk scarf Carlos had bought in a big department store downtown. She exclaimed over Maria's neatly embroidered handkerchiefs. She gave Manuel a big hug for the birthday card he had made.

Now it was Rosie's turn. First she gave Mamma the paper hat and the snaky blower. Mamma laughed and put on the hat. She blew into the blower. "We are having a real birthday party," she said.

Then Rosie handed Mamma the little red package.
"Another present?" Mamma asked. She opened the box. For a while she was too surprised to say anything more. She just stared.

"Why Rosie," she said at last, "what a wonderful, beautiful gift. I can't quite believe it. Tell me, where did you get it? Where did you get that lovely pin?"

Rosie looked around the kitchen table. They were all looking at her. They were all waiting for an answer. It was such a long story, but Rosie knew just where to begin.

"Well," she said. "First I found a button. . . ."